Nabila's Garden

Loss, Love, Heartbreak and Redemption

POEMS *by*

Hawa Fuseini

In the name of Allah,
most gracious, most merciful.
May Allah (Allah *translated as* one God Supreme Being)
forgive me for my shortcomings in this poetry
collection. May Allah forgive those who misinterpret the
meaning of the words. May Allah protect your hearts and
may he open your hearts to receive the words in this poetry
collection with love. May the words in this collection last in
your hearts forever. By Allah's grace I pray you are inspired
to become a better believer and person than you were
before reading Nabila's Garden. This poetry collection is a
book of fiction not including historical events which have
occurred. However, any characters and experiences which
may be similar to people you know are creative and artistic
forms of expression.

CONTENTS

ACKNOWLEDGMENTS

I love writing, and every piece, saying, and poem in this poetry collection is dear to my heart. By the will of Allah, I wrote *Nabila's Garden* over the years, inspired by verses in the Quran, experiences, and stories of different people. Throughout this creative process, I faced a variety of challenges, which, at times, made me feel like almost giving up.

This is why I want to thank those who supported me throughout this journey. I want to thank Allah SWT for blessing me. I cannot show enough gratitude for the blessings Allah has bestowed on my life. I want to thank my parents for motivating me to reach my full potential.

I want to thank my brother, Habib Fuseini, for offering input and advice whenever I asked him. I want to thank Chioma Okafor for motivating me and being my sounding board whenever I needed her support. I want to thank Alisha, Naima, and Fatia for keeping their word to me. I want to thank all my teachers and professors who supported me by telling me they believed I was talented or by offering their professional advice.

I want to thank Marwa Balkar for reviewing my book, and I want to thank Natalie Sheau for creating the beautiful cover. Also, last but not least, I want to thank all the Muslims around the world who are supporters of my poetry: May Allah reward you abundantly. I pray that everyone who reads this book receives blessings and love.

INTRODUCTION

Nabila Obeyere is a beautiful sixteen-year-old Muslim girl, from the Hausa tribe in Northern Nigeria. She is the daughter of the head chief in her village and Islamic scholar Uthman Obeyere. She migrated to the United States with her immigrant parents, 'Uthman and Mariam, fleeing from the corruption in Nigeria, and seeking a safe haven from the terrorist group, Boko Haram. Nabila dreamed to come to America to get an education at an Ivy League university, and help her people back home in Nigeria. However, her dream became a nightmare when she arrived in New York City, as she realized the war on Islam was constant and overwhelming. When Nabila arrived in the United States, she realized she had to face Islamophobia and racism simultaneously. Her father, 'Uthman, who was a scholar of Islam began preaching against the terrorist groups Boko Haram, Hamas and ISIS when he arrived in New York City. 'Uthman was constantly under surveillance by the FBI because he founded an organization which exposed the flaws in the American foreign policy that relates to Nigeria and the

Middle East. One day, when 'Uthman decided to travel home to Nigeria, he was abducted and killed by Boko Haram. The death of Nabila's father caused Nabila and her mother, Mariam, to face great hardship, and pain. Simultaneously, in her new high school, Nabila faced bullying from her peers because of her religion and Nigerian heritage. Amid her frustrations, lack of self-esteem, and the loss of her father, came a Muslim boy in school named Ahmad. Ahmad began to instill confidence in Nabila by showering her daily with compliments and romantically wooing her. Ahmad revealed to Nabila that he was romantically interested in her but she believed romance outside the realm of marriage was prohibited in Islam. Ahmad promised to marry Nabila if she gave him a chance but Nabila was resistant. However, Ahmad's persistence made her eventually accept his offer. Ahmad and Nabila eventually formed a relationship, but when she found out he had a secret, arranged marriage from birth with a woman in another country, her heart was broken. The struggle in Nabila's life became more than she could bear, and when she believed her life could not become worse a strange man who saw Nabila in hijab pushed her in the street downtown NY and a car hit her. Pedestrians in downtown Manhattan rushed to help Nabila, and called the police to report the hate crime, but the criminal fled the scene. The crash was horrific and the collision between the vehicle and Nabila's head knocked her out unconscious. As Nabila was rushed to the hospital, she fell into a coma. While Nabila was in this coma, she had a very long dream that she had run away to a garden in a far-away land, where no one could find her. She lived in this garden away from the reality of the world, and wrote every day, as if she were writing in her diary about her heartbreak, loss, love and finding her blessed path to Allah SWT.

Why I Write

I'm writing as if
God put this pen and paper
In my hand
Opening my mind to words
I can't even understand

I'm writing for the earthquake
That occurred in Japan
I'm writing for the poverty
and starvation in Sudan

I'm writing for my father
Who was murdered in Nigeria
I'm writing for the Civil War
that is drastically destroying Syria

I'm writing for the truth
Not being seen by the blind
I'm writing for the injustice
Taking place in Palestine

I'm writing for the girl
That doesn't know where to start because
Every boy that she's been
With left her with a broken heart

I'm writing for the blessed ones

I'm writing for the cursed
I'm writing like Charles Dickens
For the best of times and the worst

Why does wrong look right?
Why does right look wrong?
Why can't people pay attention
To the truth all along?

I'm writing for the people
Who are scared to be strong
I'm writing from morning to noon
Until dawn

I'm writing for the single mother
Who is crying until she bleeds
Because she just lost her job
and she has no money to feed

I'm down on both knees begging
My creator please
Cure the disease
and bless others to believe

The poem entitled, "Why I write," depicts the passion that Nabila has for writing and illustrating the world. This poem highlights the myriad of conflicts which occur in the world, and how they have affected Nabila. "Why I write" was written to provide the reader with a clear understanding of why Nabila writes. She writes for the sake of Allah, and because she believes the world is a place better understood when illuminated by poetry.

II LOSS

I Can't Breathe

It's hard for me to breathe
Because each breathe is a thought process
Which inhibits my mind, soul, and heart

Apart they dissect your appearance and
Together they make you a part of me
In my mind you are still alive
but reality kills me every time it hits me.

I can't breathe because you are not with me.
Your death took each breathe of mine swiftly
faster than death.
I'm at rest but R.I.P to my chest which was the
home of my heart
but inside it is cold and dark because we are apart

My diaphragm pushes my stomach
Which is lacking the love we shared
Every time you were near me
My pharynx has speechless words stuck in my
Throat because we are not close
I can't breathe because you are not with me to cope

This poem illustrates Nabila's innermost feelings regarding the loss of her father. Similar to Nabila, many times we feel lost when we lose a loved one, and coping with loss is one of our most difficult challenges in life. The poem reads, "I can't breathe because you are not with me to cope." The misconception that I believe we have is that we need people to cope with our loss. Sometimes we feel the only way to deal with loss is to hope and pray that what we lost will come back again. A good way to deal with loss is to mourn and remain steadfast in our relationship with Allah. As Nabila travels through life, and understanding loss, she allows herself to mourn and strives to become more attached to her Creator. The death of Nabila's father makes her have a strong desire to have a male figure in her life, and she really misses the bond she had with her father.

II *Dear Father*

Dear Father I don't understand
You were the man in my life
That showed me life's command
I remember the days at the beach
When we use to place our feet in the sand

Remember how you use to eat fufu
With light soup, cassava and yam?
Remember when mommy use to bring
You water for you to wash with your hands?

I remember when you use to tell me
Stories about your path to Islam.
Now I am in need of guidance
and direction towards Allah's plan

Because my heart is filled with regret
And my Iman is fighting to stand
Because while losing you I feel I am losing me
And I can't understand

The last time we said goodbye and my
fingers slipped away from your palm
I could hear my voice whispering: "don't go"
In order for me to feel calm

I know this is hard for me to accept
but Allah's knowledge is best
I pray that Allah blesses your soul and your
good deeds he accepts

I pray that you live a life in paradise and
Your soul he protects so that in the afterlife
Our souls reunite and our hearts reconnect

The loss of Nabila's father is the turning point in Nabila's life. As a young teenager, she is learning the value of life because, through her father's death, she realizes that life is not promised. Nabila reflects on the loving relationship she had with her father and she begins to struggle to understand death. Her first place of solace is in the remembrance of Allah, and she finds comfort in praying to Allah about her father. The death of Nabila's father makes her struggle with her Iman and faith; however, she continues to be steadfast and to depend on Allah, even after the loss of her father.

III NABILA'S GARDEN

Nabila's Love Garden

I could not wait until I was married
Hardship and family pressure was becoming
A huge burden to carry

All I ever wanted was a man to love me
For who I truly was
Because when I looked in the mirror I never felt
I was enough

My reflection led to my disgust
My self-esteem was always crushed
Until I met a guy in class named Ahmad
Who always seemed to make me blush

Ahmad told me I am beautiful
Ahmad told me I am smart
Ahmad's words are so vain they
Circulated through my heart

Everyday there was a spark
I knew Ahmad was the one
Even when my days were dark
I knew Ahmad was the sun and
I knew the moon was blue
When Ahmad came into my life
Because everything else was going

Wrong I never seemed to make things right

Now I had butterflies dancing in my
stomach through the night
I knew Ahmad was my light and I was
Soon to be his wife

Ahmad promised to make me happy
Ahmad promised me he would marry me
Until one stormy night
I found out Ahmad was arranged to
Marry Valerie

This arrange led to my insanity
It is pain mixed in reality
I was ashamed I allowed a man
To attain my heart without a plan for me

but maybe this was Allah's
Way of reviving my Iman for me
Because who knows who I would have
Loved most if Ahmad would have
Chose to marry me.

_____

Iman is belief in every aspect of God and Islam with
reason and action.

The poem, "Nabila's Love Garden," allows the reader to travel through her mind and her heart and feel her love for Ahmad. In this poem, the reader can tell that Nabila is looking for a man to fill the void in her heart. This is a common, dangerous mistake that many people make. Ahmad seems to be Nabila's hero in her journey to redemption after the loss of her father. However, in this poem, Ahmad disappoints Nabila, and he shows her that you can never make anyone the center of your universe, and you can never make anyone other than Allah fill the void in your heart. A human being will always disappoint you if you love that human being more than you love Allah. When we feel disappointed, it is usually because our expectations were not met. We feel hurt, due to making our imagination a reality, when our reality was merely a fantasy of our desires. When people do not fulfill our desires, this leads to disappointment and pain. We feel betrayal, and experiencing betrayal over and over again can change the way we view relationships and people forever. A part of us dies as a result of betrayal, and many dream to feel alive again.

III *Lotus Leaf*

Water did not stain the lotus leaf
The way your words did not stain
My lonely heart

Your words were encapsulated
With sin and desire
So when I made dua to Allah
Your sweet words broke apart

We envision emulating angels in the sky
But they may have flew in between
Your lips and mine

Immortal energy was essential
For preventing your evil realm
From destroying the order of
The divine

Dua can be roughly translated as supplicating or calling
out to God.

I love this poem. A lotus leaf is a beautiful leaf and the mention of it in Nabila's Garden is meant to give the reader a vivid imagery scene of her garden. I love this poem because it captures the imagery of the garden, and it depicts the dissolution of the love between Nabila and Ahmad. Nabila mentions how she prayed to Allah, and this caused the sweet words that Ahmad once told her not to have meaning to her anymore. The differentiation between lust and love is a very difficult concept for people to understand. Nabila shows that sweet words and flattery are pleasing to the ear; however, they are not always the true depiction of real love. The segment of the poem that reads, "Your words were encapsulated with sin and desire," displays the lust that Ahmad had for Nabila. This can show that sweet words and flattery are not always genuine, and that we should be careful not to confuse flattery with honest affection.

III *Dark Skin*

In Nigeria dark skin is celebrated,
Elevated, and demonstrated
In America dark skin is hated, degraded and
Castrated

Someone told me I have dark skin,
and then said I have a big gap
Is being dark skin a sin?
Do I have to repent for that?

I thought they wanted to play tic tac toe
When they said I needed a tic tac
but I saw no X's and O's on paper
So I needed to sit back

When tears began to fall
I just couldn't resist that
I know African girls are beautiful
but they are afraid to admit that

The poem entitled, "Dark skin," emotionally dives into Nabila's mind and how she feels when people tease her for her predominantly African features. This is a period of time in Nabila's life that negatively impacts her self-esteem and body image. Nabila feels she is not considered beautiful, when people make fun of her dark skin. She does not know how to respond to people when they scrutinize her skin color, and make her feel bad about her physical appearance. In this piece, she states that she knows African women are beautiful, but they are afraid to admit that. This segment of the poem shows that Nabila understands the physical features common on African women are what are considered ugly or unattractive, but she still strives to have self-confidence by reminding herself that African women are beautiful, even though the people around her do not acknowledge it. Still, the bullying affects her self-esteem. Nabila strives to believe Allah created her beautifully and that she does not need validation from human beings.

III *Rag Head*

Today in class a boy
Called me a rag head
Baghdad head
Wearing a hijab for my
Dad head

So Would I be wrong
If I called him a crack head?
or if I would have popped
Him quicker than a blackhead?

When they scream terrorist
I am telling you that's dead
Count the dead bodies on Muslim
Soil if you want to see where terror
Has led

If my ink can spill of their blood
I am telling you it's that red
You have more dirt in your heart
than the mud and you call me a rag head?

I do not intend to incite violence by writing the poem entitled, "Rag head." I do not condone violence. The purpose of this poem was to highlight a common, underlying event, which occurs to Muslims living in America as a result of Islamophobia. I also believe it is every Muslim's duty to promote the peace, which Islam stands for, and also to be conscientious of our actions and how our actions affect people and the society in which we live. I also believe that, in the United States, Muslims should be able to exercise their constitutional rights, which include freedom of religion, as long as our actions do not harm or physically endanger other American citizens. From a personal perspective, to call someone a *rag head* is to demean and disrespect their free religious choice to wear the hijab. In this poem, Nabila shows how being called a *rag head* infuriates her and makes her want to retaliate by saying the wrong words back. However, Nabila decides not to respond with hate because she wants to be a good Muslim and she knows responding with hate would not help her to evolve into a better person. If people want to be respected for their beliefs, they should also respect the beliefs of others.

III *America is Great*

Lights flashing in my eyes
Feeling I'm becoming blind
Wondering if I am alive
My Heart is beating quickly inside

Pedestrians pick me from the depths
Call the cops there was a threat
Car hit me near to my death

My mother is angry and upset
Because If you hit a black Muslima
You might not have to face arrest.

"America is Great," is a poem which uses a slogan to depict the ideas some people have pertaining to making America great again. The phrase, "Let's Make America Great Again," has been popularized by Donald Trump and it is a slogan which displays solidarity at the cost of other marginalized groups of people. In this poem the slogan is said at the same time that Nabila is pushed into the street by a terrorist. Nabila becomes the victim of a hate crime because Islam has been associated with terrorism and she portrays herself as a Muslim girl by wearing the hijab which makes her an easy target. Nabila is hit by a car after she is pushed into the street, and this is a very traumatic experience for her. Shortly after, Nabila falls into a coma and begins to imagine herself in a garden writing poems which reflect on her life, love, and relationship with Allah swt.

III *Coma Leaves*

Awakening to a sea of black
With harsh breeze
and Harsh trees

In a beautiful garden
Even though
It is hard to breathe

and I do not know when the coma leaves
but this is my time to find peace
My time to find love
My time to find ease

This is a time when Nabila is in a coma and she has a vivid scene in her mind. Nabila feels more peaceful because she is escaping from all the problems in her life. She is not suffering when she is in this state. She is actually feeling at peace because she is able to reflect on her life, love, and loss, and strive towards her path of redemption.

III *Dreams on a Rose*

Plucking petals
But he loves me not
So I dream on a rose

I dream one day I will be loved
I dream one day you will be close
I dream there will a come time
You will really love me the most

I dream one day you
will not desert me and
I dream one day you will never hurt me
Sometimes dreams are not what they seem
And then reality comes and I feel like someone
cursed me

I have dreams of love on a rose
Not dreams on a bed
Because a bed is not alive but
A rose can survive long before it is dead

"Dreams on a Rose" is a poem which shows how Nabila feels for Ahmad, but she realizes she is dreaming and that she needs to eventually wake up and practice the *deen* sincerely. She knows she needs to repent to Allah and focus on her relationship with Allah SWT. She still struggles with her *desires*, but she is also aware that she has to make wise decisions if she wants to protect her *faith in God*.

III *Beautiful Garden*

How dare you allow men to plant
Seeds in your garden
Just because they said they loved it?

What if farmers allowed strangers?
To plant seeds into their gardens
Just because they said they loved it?

Wouldn't the community starve and die?
Because you would allow strangers to eat all of
The fruits in your garden just so you can keep them
alive?

They can't nurture their seeds
So they to pretend to bear fruits in your garden
So they can pluck them and leave

Their hearts are filled with greed
No care for their communities
So the communities starve and die
When all the fruits are gone
Because you allowed a stranger to eat all the fruits in
your beautiful garden just so you could keep him alive

When your children are dying of hunger
You tell them you gave all your fruits to a stranger
Just because he said he loved it
When your children ask: Mommy where are the men
that love you?

We are dying of hunger?
Tell them that mommy is a fool she thought the rain
Would come just because she heard the thunder
Tell your children

Those strangers
Think love is the desire to
Touch. Grab. Eat. Then Leave.

Tell them they don't know
Love is watering your seeds
To grow healthy family trees

Tell them they don't know
Because they have never been taught
Why would they want to grow family trees when
They see other men stealing fruits from your beautiful
garden and they never get caught?

Tell your children you allowed strangers to eat all of
your fruits just because they said they loved it
Tell them why they are dying of hunger
Tell them it is because mommy is a fool
She thought the rain would come just because she hea
rd the thunder.

The poem entitled "Beautiful Garden," utilizes a metaphor for a woman's body and womb. The purpose of this poem is to make women reflect on past mistakes, or to inspire women to be dignified in their choices before allowing men into their lives. This poem is not meant to force beliefs on anyone; however; it is meant to highlight the effects of allowing anyone in our lives. When we are cautious and selective with who we allow into our garden, we can avoid pain and heartbreak. Also, not being selective about who you allow into your garden can give people the chance to leave behind thorn bushes, which hurt us instead of roses and beautiful, green grass, which help us to grow. This poem is also not meant to take away the responsibility from men to be morally upright; nevertheless, it is focused on women.

IV JIHAD AL-NAFS

Sick Heart

I never want to answer to
The whispers of Satan when
No one is looking and
I never want to wake up
Twenty minutes late for Fajr and not care

I never want to desire to be held by anything
Other than Allah's words and
I never want to stare in the mirror
For hours desiring to take off my hijab

In order to fit in with the rest of society
or desire to take a selfie without hijab
To get likes on Facebook

I never want to desire to turn up
or get high with my peers
or feel the need to disobey Allah
In order to make his creation happy

I never want to do a good deed
Only to be seen by men and not by Allah
I never want to have my heart
Filled with so much sin

That I can no longer cry when I hear
The recitation of the Qur'an

I never want to have a heart
So sick

That I believe I am perfectly fine
and that I do not need repentance
To Allah as my medication

Most of us do not reflect on whether
We have a sick heart
I never want to have a sick heart

I want to leave this dunya with a heart
So pure

Allah will send down
A million angels
To carry my dying parts

Dunya meaning lowly or referring to the temporary world.

Fajr is the prayer at dawn.

Quran is the holy Islamic book.

Hijab Islamic dress code to promote modesty, and dignity.

The poem, "Sick Heart," illustrates the battle of the desires faced by many people all around the world. When Nabila arrives in the United States, she is faced with many challenges and temptations, which she struggles to overcome. The temptations she faces are outlined in the poem, and she does not want to give in to any of them.

She motivates herself to be steadfast by reminding herself of the reward of obeying God. She also speaks of the ill effects of having a sick heart, which can be desiring what is *prohibited*. Not only does Nabila want to avoid committing sins, but also she does not even want to desire to sin, because, to her, this would mean that her heart is not pure.

IV *This Love is a Sin*

I've been waiting
For your text all night
and I didn't get it

I need to pray
Qiyam al layl
and hope that I forget it

I need to beg Allah
To place me where I need to be
Because when I'm at my best
Is the only time that
You want to speak to me

As soon as my head touches the prayer mat
Is when you reach for me
But I know Allah loves me more than you
So rushing through prayer to speak to you
Will never be complete for me

Sometimes thinking about the afterlife
Can get too deep for me
I start to think about
If I will get punished
For my indecency

I start to think of various ways
That I can clean up my intentions
Instead of thinking of ways to clean up
My appearance so I can get your attention

Because I know only through
Allah's mercy will I ever win and

If acknowledging my bad actions
Is a good deed then

This love is a sin.

Jihad translated from Arabic to English as the spiritual struggle against oneself or sin.

Qiyam al layl is the night prayer.

The poem, "This love is a sin," shows Nabila's intense struggle with her desires. In the depths of the night, she struggles against sin, which is the greater form of *Jihad*, and what Nabila is facing. Nabila still has a desire to be with Ahmad, even though he broke her heart and took her away from Allah. Nabila knows that she needs to beg Allah for his mercy and forgiveness for being in a *haram* relationship with Ahmad. A part of Nabila even wants to pray to Allah to bring Ahmad back in her life, and, although this seems absurd, false love can make the human mind think about crazy solutions for the heart. She battles between her soul, mind, and heart, and seeks Allah's guidance in the process. What really makes her regret her actions are when she thinks about the punishment she will have to face when she dies and meets Allah on the Day of Judgment. Nabila acknowledges that she has to purify her intentions instead of only focusing on how to be beautiful for a man who is not her husband. She realizes her mistakes, and knows that she is not perfect, but she also knows that, through Allah's mercy, she can still be successful in the afterlife.

IV *Answered Prayer*

I'm losing sleep
My feelings are deeper
Than my thoughts have been
Ever since we have stopped talking
I have been crying often

Approaching you is what
I'm denying often
I'm just hoping that
You will notice me

As the moon orbits around the sun
I am hoping you will come close to me
I am hoping that you will never marry that woman
but that is only what I hope to be

Because only then will you understand
Being with me is how it's supposed to be
I am attached after we detached from each other

I am missing you so much
Hoping that we come back
To each other

I am a passionate lover
I am trying not to let that
Get the best of me
Because either I'm facing the
Consequences of my actions or

Allah is only testing me
Simultaneously school is stressing me
I now understand the complexity

Of your efforts for me
Hoping that one day
You will be next to me

I now understand why you prayed
For me to feel the same for you

I know that your prayer has been
Answered but I don't know if feelings
Have changed for you

I am fearing the possibility of things not
Being the same for you
Because you may forget how much you prayed but
You may never forget how the answered
Prayer came too late for you.

In the poem, "Answered Prayer," Nabila reflects on the time when Ahmad was praying that Nabila would give him a chance. She begins to regret her decisions because she believes she should have prayed to Allah to keep her steadfast when Ahmad was pursuing her romantically without proving he would marry her. Ahmad prolonged the *Nikah* (marriage) by building a trust with Nabila through lies. This is a common manipulative tactic used in relationships. Even though Ahmad has hurt her, she still cannot sleep at night, and this is one of the ill effects of loving someone in an unhealthy way. Nabila is very confused in this period of her life because she does not want to disobey Allah, but, at the same time, she misses Ahmad because he made her feel good at a time when she felt she was worthless. She says in the poem, "Because either I'm facing the consequences of my actions or Allah is only testing me." This segment of the poem shows Nabila's confusion at what is taking place in her life because she is not sure whether the heartbreak is a consequence of her actions, a test from Allah, or both. At the end of the poem, she shows that she still desires to be with Ahmad, even though she has experienced pain and betrayal. This poem shows how difficult it is to remove oneself from an impermissible relationship and truly

love Allah more than our desires. Nabila is struggling
with winning the battle against her *nafs* (desires).

IV *I Wish I Could Tell You This*

I've been thinking for hours
Rearranging the perfect words
To describe to you
Analyzing our conversations
and the number of times
I did not reply to you

When I think of love
I'm still not sure if that really
Applies to you but
When you're not around
I still have enough love in me
That makes me cry for you but
Maybe they're just my *nafs*

Maybe they're just my desires
Because I have a myriad of goals
I really need to acquire

and this distraction between our souls
Is really making me tired
I don't want to drag you
Through my problems

Too much friction creates fires
Too much addiction creates liars
Too much affliction creates criers

I would rather create something
That will not cause our love to expire

This poem shows how strong Nabila's desire to be with Ahmad is. She wastes her time thinking for hours about someone who is not even thinking about her. She speaks about how Ahmad has been contacting her, but she has not replied to him since she found out about his secret arranged marriage. Nabila knows that the relationship was *haram*, so she is not sure whether or not she truly loved Ahmad, but she does know she still desires to be with him and she cries in his absence. Nabila still wishes that Ahmad would marry her, and that their love could last forever. It seems that it will take Nabila some time before she can really move on, and not be emotionally attached to Ahmad. These poems, which focus on Nabila fighting against her *nafs*, show why it is important to stay away from *haram* relationships because the amount of confusion and pain that they cause can feel unbearable.

IV *Can't erase love*

I can erase you from my contacts but
I can't erase you from my memories
Because it seems the longer
We have been out of contact
The more I remember how much
You were a friend to me

Even if I used my eraser to erase
All the words you ever said to me
They would come back alive because
Our love was never dead to me

They come back to life when I write
They keep me up when I pretend to sleep
You left but live inside of me
So I hear your voice when I intend to speak

When I intend to make a decision
This is what your voice says to me
It says, "Kill the negativity,
Instill the positivity, pray work hard and
Show the world your real ability."

The only problem is
I don't know if you were
Really there for me
If you were able to move on so fast
How could I believe you ever cared for me?

In this poem, "Can't erase love," Nabila struggles to forget about Ahmad. Nabila has been trying to erase Ahmad from her memories, but she can't seem to stop thinking about him. The problem is that she allowed Ahmad to have a part of her heart without commitment, and now she is suffering from the consequences of her actions. Nabila allowed someone to take up more space in her heart than the person deserved, and now, since her heart is attached to Ahmad, so is her mind. This is the problematic effect of choosing anything over Allah. This eventually leads to our own detriment. The amount of time that Nabila is fighting her desire to be with Ahmad is even longer than the time that she mourned the death of her father, and this shows how deeply heartbreak can affect the human being. At times, it may seem as if a part of you has died.

Reflection

Tissues wipe away the tears
But they don't wipe away the pain
Apologies wipe away the pride
But they don't wipe away the shame

You never wiped the lies
But tried to wipe away my pain?
How could you wipe away the sky?
Before you wipe away the rain?

In another realm of the universe
Love is what we became
But in our present existence
The thought is merely insane.

The thought is merely insane
Our feelings have interchanged
You love me and I don't love you
and it hurts you I'm not the same

1000 letters burned from
The remembrance of your name
1000 tears shed from
The remembrance of the pain

In the afterlife when it is only our soul

Which remains
and our bodies have
transformed
into ashes you can
never hurt me again

This poem is a very emotional piece. It shows the reader how Nabila feels since Ahmad broke her heart. This is also a reflective piece because Nabila begins to think about all the events that occurred in her relationship with Ahmad. Nabila speaks about how Ahmad lied but also tried to show empathy after the damage to her heart was already done. Nabila explains how apologies and tissues are not enough to fix the damaged heart. This is expressed when she says, "Tissues wipe away the tears, but they don't wipe away the pain. Apologies wipe away the pride, but they don't wipe away the shame." This segment from the poem shows how Nabila feels about Ahmad's inability to do anything to make up for the pain and heartbreak he has caused her. She is also teaching the reader that before you say sorry, you should make sure that you do not do something which would warrant an apology in the first place. Nabila shows how difficult and painful heartbreak is, and how it can change the way someone views the world and relationships forever.

V *The Hurt One*

When your first one
Is the worst one
You become afraid of true love
You feel like you're the cursed one

Going to the masjid
The Khutba alerts one
Teaches you a lesson
So that you don't hurt one

Since I'm the hurt one
I tried to assert one
I tried to control the things
That I became hurt from

I was hurt from the things
I thought I could learn from
But I learned from the things
That I became hurt from

Khutba - sermon given by the imam on the day of the
Friday congregational prayer.

In the poem entitled, "The Hurt One," Nabila reflects on how a bad experience of one's first love can make one feel cursed and afraid of true love. This may be a part of why Allah prohibits secret, and haram relationships. Allah knows the damaging effects of illegitimate relationships, and there are many. Sometimes heartbreak is one of the least damaging effects of *haram* relationships. In many scenarios, people have children who are not born through true love, and they suffer the consequences of two individuals who brought children into this world irresponsibly. "The Hurt One" focuses on telling the story not only of Nabila but also of anyone whose first love was their worst love, and has now changed their view of relationships forever.

V *Untitled*

You fell in love with me through my art
Until you realized I was really as depressed
as my poems

Now you don't want my heart
You just want to leave me alone

Leaving me at a time when you
Know I need you the most

It is clear that your feelings died
and our memories became the ghost

This poem is a reflective piece about how it feels when someone loves you for materialistic reasons, such as your talent, money, status, or beauty, and the effects that this can have when the person loves you solely for these reasons. The problem is that many people love the rainbow, but not the thunder storm. Many people love diamonds, but not the pressure. This common characteristic of human beings also translates to the way we love. Many people love people because of what they have, not because of who they are. A common example of this problematic problem of our society would be the many times when people first meet you. Most people will ask you where you are from, where you live, where you work, or what do you do for a living. How different would the world be if, when the first time someone met you, they asked how you felt, what you would like to eat, what makes you happy, or what makes you sad? These questions don't often seem to be asked when we first meet someone because people appear to be mainly concerned with defining you by your wealth, beauty and social status.

V *Easy to Love Yesterday*

Yesterday I was your fantasy
That your teacher would catch you
Daydreaming about in the middle of lecture

Yesterday I was your dream
That you did not want to wake up
From but your mother would shout your name
Until you built the strength to get up from your
Cozy bed to answer her

Yesterday I was your imagination
That you described to your friends
While they played NBA 2k live causing
Them to miss the last free throw

Yesterday I was a mere thought
An abstract being that could not
Possibly be yours

Yesterday I was the woman
You valued because you did not have me
Yesterday I was only a wish and not a reality
Yesterday you would do anything
To make me yours and you would
Seek advice from your friends on
How to get me

Yesterday you would do anything
To make me happy because my smile
Radiated through your sadness

Yesterday you were crying for my attention
Yesterday you would send me messages
Hoping and praying to get a reply

Yesterday you would write me poems
Professing your love to me in order to
Prove your sincerity but

Today you say emotionally empty
One syllable words

Today you ignore me
Today you think you have me
Today I am not your fantasy
Today I am your reality and
Today you do not value me

Today you see my soul without makeup.
The snorkel in my laugh and all my imperfections
Today you see that I am not perfect and
I too need corrections

Today you see that I am not all that
you were expecting
Today you see I am a normal woman
Today you see I love too hard
Today you see I love too fast
Today you see I can be too emotional

Today I may not be what you dreamed of but
Today I realized I want someone who will truly
Love me for who I really am and
That is why you will not have a chance
To be with me tomorrow

The poem, "Easy to love yesterday," shows how fascinated a man can be with loving a woman before he has her. Many times, men and women love the fantasy they have of another person more than the real person. The fantasy is always better because it serves our desires and what we want to extract from the person we claim to love. However, when we actually get our dream spouse, some of us do not love their imperfections. At times, the imperfect parts of the people we claim to love annoy us and agitate us beyond our imagination, even though we claimed to love everything about them. Many relationships seem to fail today because of the failure to truly understand that nobody is perfect. We love the parts of people which are the farthest away from reality. We love the beauty, but hate the old age. We love the money, but hate the downfalls, which are a reality of this life. We love smooth skin, but we hate stretch marks. Sometimes the world shows how much it loves women's bodies, but hates women for their character traits and personalities. It is always easy to love yesterday because today you face the reality and yesterday is only an imaginary place of today. We easily love the fantasy and not the reality.

V *Promise of Marriage*

Before you texted me that night
I was thinking for days about
Reasons I should stay. But I knew
I needed to go.

I clinged on our memories as if
I was falling in quick sand and
You were the only one I could
Hold onto.

I believe that night before you
Texted me Shaytaan whispered
In my ear and said: "but would
Allah want you to be lonely…
Do you want to be really lonely
With no one to talk to?"

"No one is going to marry you
So you might as well hold on
To whatever you get."

But I did not care because my fear
Of Allah became greater than my
Fear of never getting married or
Dying alone and I knew Allah was
Calling me back to him.

I bit my lips while peeling my skin
Off quickly thinking about how life
Would be for me if I was to die
Anytime soon.

I thought about how you would not
Be with me in the grave to comfort
My soul with your lust filled I love you's

How the butterflies you gave me in my
Stomach could not spread their wings
And fly me to Jannah.

I thought about how your rope stitched with
Promises of marriage stretched over the years

Without you tying the knot.

"Do you know how much I love you?" You asked
Me over the phone with silence between each
Promise which almost made me believe you meant
The words you coughed up through your lips.

That was the easiest way to keep me trapped in
Your forest with trees that grew from lack of
Faith and fruits of desires which you ate every
time I lacked the strength to escape.

I was fooled with the way you made me feel good
and confused it with being in love but it was autumn
and your branches of lies were not helping me grow
So I needed to leave you.

I knew I needed to reflect on the
Verse in Surah Nisa [4:25] in which Allah
States: "You [believers] are of one another.
So marry them with the permission of their
People and give them their due compensation

According to what is acceptable.
They should be chaste, neither of
Those who commit unlawful intercourse
Randomly nor those who take secret lovers."

Allah revealed to me clearly how much you

Loved me and that is exactly why I had to go
Because you did not love me enough to care
About my akhira.

You did not love me enough to marry me in
This dunya and you did not love me enough
To help me preserve my Iman.

After hanging up the phone and blocking you
I cried because I wanted to be strong but at
The same time I wanted to be loved and being
Stuck between two opposite poles pulling me
Back and forth was far too much.

I began to worry about how I lost a friend of me
But then I remembered how on the day of judgement
The friends who took us farther away from Allah
Would turn into our enemies.

Akhira translated as the Islamic term for afterlife.

Surah Nisa chapter four in the *Holy Qur'an*

Dunya lowly or referring to the worldly life

"Promise of marriage," dives into the problem that many youth face. Nabila displays how much trust she placed in Ahmad. She really believed Ahmad would marry her merely because he said he would. The mistake that Nabila made that many, especially young, Muslim girls, make, when it comes to relationships, is believing a man will marry them, even though he has not taken the steps according to the Quran and Sunnah to prove he is sincere. Many young women believe the words of boys, who promise they will marry them, but they just need a little more time. She should ask herself why someone who wants something very badly would need more time. Ask yourself if you were to offer this person money right now if you think they would say they needed more time before deciding whether they wanted to take the money from you or not. That shows you, and proves to you, that the person you trust does not value you. Why would you want to be with someone who values something as fleeting and materialistic, as money, or bragging rights, more than you, just because you are lonely? May Allah protect us.

Sunnah can be translated as the teachings and lifestyle of the Prophet Muhammad (peace be upon him).

V *The Check Up*

The doctor suggested
That I cut sugar out of my diet
So I decided to cut you out of my life
Because your sweet words made me sick
and you never tried to be quiet

I suggest that you should try it.
You should try to be more organic.
Take in things that will help you become
A better person on this planet

Because you're a person causing
Damage consuming things that are processed
Your words are artificially modified and your
Intentions are out of context

I advise men and women to not consume
Things without reading the content because
I ate sweet words that hurt me because
They seemed convenient

But next time I will not ingest love
Without checking the ingredients.

"The Check Up" explores the growth in Nabila's understanding because she realizes that she needs to stop listening to Ahmad's sweet words, which have no substance. She realizes that sweet words and flattery can actually cause harm when we accept them without questioning the sincerity behind them. In fact, when you keep listening to these sweet words for a long period of time, you can become addicted. Nabila advises other people, based on her experience, that they should not accept flattery just because it makes you feel good, but you should think about why someone is using flattery to appeal to you. You should not simply absorb all the compliments you receive without thinking about whether the person giving the compliment is saying it sincerely, or only to extract something from you. Nabila promises herself that she will never again accept love until she is sure the person wants to commit to her through marriage, and she knows exactly what the person means by the phrase, "I love you."

V *The race*

I was chasing you but never catching you
We were racing and I was in back of you and
These races came in different faces and mine was
Just not attracting you.

During lonely nights...I tried to fight
My soul that was attached to you and
While I was after you
I prayed I would never desire to come
back to you but

I was battling my nafs
I was battling my mind
I was battling and chasing after a love
I never seemed to find because

No matter how fast I ran
You always left me behind
and I was so slow I realize I
never won you over after you left me
at the finish line.

"The race" explores Nabila's emotions and captures her feelings during her reflection on her heartbreak. She embodies raw emotion in an attempt to illustrate her feelings of regret. The poem uses metaphors such as running to show how Nabila chased relentlessly after Ahmad, and she still did not get his true love. Nabila chased Ahmad, even after he told her he had an arranged marriage with another girl. When we are hurt by someone we love, we commonly seem to still chase after them because we fear how our life will be when that person is no longer in our lives. We need to fear how our life will be if we lose our relationship with Allah. However, many of us know we need to love Allah most, and yet we still allow our hearts to become attached to things other than Allah, and when these other things fail us, we become disappointed. "The race" illustrates how many of us run after things relentlessly, such as love and people, and these things still leave us behind, no matter how fast we run after them.

V *Empty Heart*

A tornado in my mind
A hurricane in the dark
All I hear is the thunder now
and I'm stuck with an empty heart

I thought I was never blind
Thought I never needed a candle sparked but
If I was blessed with a wish
I would wish for a blossomed heart

I want butterflies to fly
I want roses to bud and sprout
For hours I've been trying to cry
And dry tears have been coming out

When I focus on purification
Instead of on only what I can gain
I realize I am Allah's creation and
My distance from him
Is why I'm feeling the pain

I know if I fall deeper in love with Allah
I will be released from these chains
In the Garden of Paradise where rivers flow
I pray my soul will remain.
Ameen

The poem, "Empty Heart," reflects on Nabila's experience as she strives to let go of all the false attachments in her life. "Empty Heart" embodies Nabila's emotions, when she is fighting to let go of false love, mourning over her father's death, and striving to build her relationship with Allah. An important step to take when one is striving to get closer to Allah is to stop committing the sin that is killing our relationship with Allah. While we are letting go of our desires, we can feel empty inside and lonely. When we feel empty, the way to fill ourselves is to fall deeper in love with Allah.

VI REPENTANCE

VI *Prayer to Allah*

I call on you to cure my diseases
and you never get sick of me
As much as I ask from you
You still do not add up all of the
Things that you did for me

Because you solve problems differently
It's a different thing
To be in the room alone
Wishing I had someone close to me but

In the Quran you told me you are closer
To me than my jugular veins
"We are closer to him than his jugular vein" [50:16]
So this is the way things are supposed to be

The angels record my good and bad deeds
I pray that my bad deeds are forgiven hopefully
And when I close my eyes to sleep and you take

My soul at night
I pray that you purify
My soul for me

"Prayer to Allah" is a poem that displays gratitude to Allah and shows Nabila's way of seeking repentance. The poem describes how Nabila feels she has done so much wrong, but she still receives help and mercy from Allah. This is an inspirational piece, which allows the reader to see from another perspective how merciful Allah is. The poem reads, "I ask you to cure all of my diseases and you never get sick of me," showing Nabila's appreciation for Allah's mercy.

VI *Far Away*

Allah I'm so far away
and I feel my heart is away
Some wish upon a star
I wish upon your mercy and pray

Because we've been apart for some days
We were apart from some years
But you consoled me when I was down
and when I was lonely with tears

I've been alone with these tears
And I've been feeling nonexistent
Then in flew in ~~Influenza~~ the sickness
and suffocation from the distance

"Verily, in the remembrance of Allah
Do hearts find rest" 13:28
Verily, in true love do our hearts reconnect?
My heart is upset

But yet,
My mind is focused on building trust
Since I've been breaking down
I've been focused on building up

And I *really just*
Want to be *religious*
Tell the truth
Fight for peace
and be
Really just

This poem is a reflective piece about feeling far away from Allah. This poem reflects the emotional feelings of Nabila because of the hardship in her life. It is easy to feel far away from Allah when life is getting difficult for us. We easily feel as though Allah does not care about us. The challenge many of us fail to overcome is actually remaining patient during our difficult times, and being dedicated enough to never lose hope and faith. When we are persistent and never lose hope in Allah, we will not fail. Allah stated in the Quran in Chapter 50, Verse 16, that, "We are nearer to him than his jugular vein." Allah already told us that he is very close to us, so we should never feel Allah is far away from us.

VI *In Jannah*

Do you dream of the day
You may see Allah?
and wake up in paradise
With gardens and rivers that flow
In Jannah?

Do you dream of traveling to
Jannah to play?
Where all of your problems
Go away?
A place you can always
Stay.

Do you dream of praying
Next to Aisha ra and Khadijah ra?
and sharing the most blessed words
With the most blessed teachers?

Do you dream of having the most
Beautiful features?
A face that shines with Noor
A soul that shines with the
Believers?

Do you dream of feeling

Safe, loved and adorned?
A place where you are cherished
Hugged, and adorned?

This dream can become reality

If we pray and seek repentance more
In Jannah
I pray that we one day
Explore.

Some of us think of Jannah as far away, and this can make some people procrastinate when it comes to performing good deeds and dedicating our lives to Allah SWT. In this poem, Nabila is depicted as dreaming about being in Jannah. This is Nabila's dream. Nabila is not aware that she is in a coma at this point, and she is dreaming of where she wants her final destination to be, which is with Allah. She has an intense dream and desire to feel loved, and Nabila believes she will receive the true love she is searching for only in Jannah.

VII ENLIGHTENMENT

VII *Allah is Protecting Us*

What if I wrote on the wings of birds?
That could fly to your destination?
and as they flew across the sky
They recited the revelation?

And as the sun came out
It filled the dark crevices
In your soul with illumination?
Would this kill the doubts in your Iman?
and guide you to fall in prostration
To Allah and not the creation?

Would it cause contemplation?
Would your soul come alive again or
Would it cause it to die again?
As soon as the birds left the sky again?

At times when the sun goes
We know it can rise again
So why is it that when we feel down
We feel we will never feel high again

There is no stability in this *dunya*
So when we fall we have to rise again

It hurts but what is worse is when we fall
But we do not rely on him

Allah is our protector
and trusting in him is essential
So do not trust in other people
Who do not realize your full potential

We all want to fly
But our fear of falling
Is what is preventing us
The day we fly
Is the day that we realize
That Allah is protecting us

The poem, "Allah is Protecting Us," emphasizes that we, as human beings, should depend on Allah, and trust that he is protecting us. Many of us struggle with believing that Allah is protecting us and that he would not burden our souls with more than they can bear (2:286). Allah loves those who put their trust in him (3:159). Our love for Allah and the trust we place in Allah only benefits us. I believe one of the best ways to cure our sadness is to listen to the recitation of the Qur'an. The poem reads that "our fear of falling is what is preventing us. The day we fly is the day we realize that Allah is protecting us." This segment from the poem is not meant to be taken literally; however, it is meant to highlight the importance of trusting in Allah. There will be times in your life when you will realize that, no matter what you do, you do not have control over the outcome of situations. This is the time when we have to make a decision to seek Allah's guidance, and decide whether we will truly place all of our trust in Allah SWT.

VII *Allah Truly Loves Her*

Sinning and still asking
For his protection
You would think if she did not win
She would finally learn her lesson

But she finally learned not to question
Why Allah made certain things wrong for us
He created our hearts inside
Knowing the outside world
Would be strong enough

To cage in our desires
Filled with rage
And burning fire
In the grave she still
A slave

To the possessions
She did not acquire
Unless her intention was to aspire
To become a better believer
To fly over the temptations of this world
Like the temptations are beneath her

With the strength Allah gave her
The devil could not defeat her
and with the sense Allah blessed her with
Society could not deceive her

Allah truly loves her
That is why he instilled beauty in her deen
Embodied her with self esteem
Even a magazine cover could not pressure

her to desire to be seen

Women have lost the definition of
What womanhood really means
We have been created and degraded into products
Instead of being elevated as human beings

But because she serves the greatest
Allah loves and protects her from what is haram
She has been gifted and blessed with the protection of
Allah

This poem reflects on Nabila's ability to self-reflect on her relationship with Allah. Nabila realized that she was still sinning, and, even though her sins were to no avail, she still did not learn her lesson after suffering the consequences of her sins. The main issue in this poem is that Nabila would sin, but when she was in need, she would then ask Allah for his protection before repenting. This is not befitting for anyone. We should not only call on Allah when we are in need. Also, even though Nabila sins, Allah makes her realize her actions are *haram* by making her suffer the consequences in this life through heartbreak and disappointment. This is actually a blessing in disguise. Allah truly loves her and that is why, when she does wrong, she feels the pain and guilt in her heart. The pain and guilt we feel after committing a sin is a sign that what we are doing is wrong. This is actually a blessing from Allah that we should appreciate

VII *Garden of faith*

Do we live in an era?
Where faith exists
In a mix of balled up fists
With souls dying in their hands
Hoping the truth will never depict?

Does the truth hold a grip on their tongues?
Escape as lies through our eyes
And reside as nicotine in our lungs?

If the truth is the disease
and the lies are the medication
How can the youth be at ease
and follow the revelation?

We are living in a critical situation because
All day we are bombarded with immorality and
degradation
Five minute prayers for spiritual stimulation
Is this the strength of our faith?

Is it in the Western World's hand?
Or do we hide the teachings of the Qur'an from our
actions because we are in the Western World's land?

What era are we living in?
Are we in imprisonment?
If you were to die tonight
Which state would you be risen in?

In the poem, "Garden of faith," you can understand that Nabila is attempting to wake up humanity. She asks rhetorical questions in order to get people to start thinking about what is going on with our faith, and to inspire people to revive their *faith*. She focuses on targeting our era and our contemporary times in order to help us to think about our current problems. She asks questions such as, "Is this the strength of our faith?" "What state would you be risen in?" Nabila uses an appeal to logic and emotion to help people by waking them up and stirring up emotion. She enlightens the reader by informing the reader that we are continuously bombarded with immorality; however, we may only spend five minutes praying to Allah. How will our hearts be pure, when we are constantly exposed to filth, and we spend only a little of our time praying to the one who can purify our hearts?

VII *Blind eyes that can see*

Who are we today as people?
We barely want to be considered equal
Setting ourselves by classes...
The rich and the poor
Causing clashes

Calling war a heroic act.
How much more blind can we get?
Are we on this earth to torment and stress?
Or to serve our lord...be mindful and progress

We need to think outside the box
and open our eyes ...stop looking
At what we don't have and appreciate
What we've got.

Time is ticking check your clock
What we have to do is change figure
Out what is good and leave the remains

Racism is something we have to stop
Politicians in the western world have to stop
Lying to us like were a play top
We're spinning and spinning but we have no
Inclination of our surroundings so we just drop

We have to open our eyes and realize
That it is open minded that you have to be
So that our blind eyes can see

"Blind eyes that can see" is a piece in which Nabila channels her frustration and loss of her father during his trip to Nigeria. The death of Nabila's father makes her despise war and violence even more. She sees war and violent acts as a path to destruction. The poem reads, "Calling war a heroic act. How much more blind can we get?" This segment from the poem shows Nabila's view of war, and it allows the reader to understand the damage of war from Nabila's perspective. The poem is entitled "Blind eyes that can see," because although we can physically see, we are still blind to the matters of the world. We live our lives as if we are sleep-walking, and we do as we are told without asking critical questions in order to find out the truth.

VII *Spoils of War*

You buried broken hearts and then
Watered them down with lies so the
Truth escaped

This is where you told little black
Girls their fate
Told them who they will never grow
Until they believe with faith

That their purpose in life is beyond
Marriage
Their purpose in life is to serve the most Great

Because if Mary did not have to marry in order to
have a blessed son
Then why do I have to marry in order to know
That I am a blessed one?

The poem, "Spoils of War," focuses on a battle in Nabila's mind that she engages in after her heart is broken by Ahmad. Nabila mentions how Ahmad buried her broken heart. This means that Ahmad disregarded how much he hurt Nabila, and pushed his detrimental actions under the rug. Ahmad's decision to undermine the pain he caused Nabila has caused fruits of hate to grow. Nabila expresses how she feels hate and resentment towards Ahmad. There are symbolic elements used throughout this piece in order to express, in a creative way, the effects of lies, heartbreak, and pressure on women to get married before they are considered valuable to society.

VIII SELF-ESTEEM

Only a Matter of Time

Have you ever questioned if you matter?
Not questioned if your mass that takes up space.
But have you ever questioned if your existence
Plays a central role in this place?

So many people called me a nobody
That I wanted to do anything to mean
Something to somebody

Because anyone can say they love you
Through a text but not everyone will hug
You when you feel depressed
Not everyone will stand by you
When you are stressed

But most people will say you do not matter
When you have less and everyone will say they
Believed in you when you are at your best

But you will still feel as though you do not matter
Because knowing people love you for what you
Have and not who you are makes you sadder

The poem, "Only a Matter of Time," shows how bullying someone and making them feel irrelevant can negatively impact their self-esteem and self-worth. The more someone hears from other people that they are a nobody or that they are not important, the more likely that person is to believe it. It will only be a matter of time before that person questions if their presence on this earth matters at all. Many people think of suicide because they feel worthless and because they feel they do not matter to anyone. It is the tongue, at times, which can be our sharpest weapon, and we need to be careful about how we decide to use it.

VIII *Power of Hijab*

You ask her to take off her hijab
Will that make her prettier?
Or will that shift your focus from her
Interior to her exterior

What intimidates you most?
A woman that walks with confidence?
A woman that does not need to objectify
Herself or have her value based upon
Your disingenuous compliments?

I know at times it seems tough when
You want to receive some acknowledgment
Except when you realize the love of Allah
Is far more astonishing

There's something special about your determination
To wait for the right attention.
With trust in Allah you will attract people in your life
With the right intentions.

Don't tell a Muslim woman to take it off
Because she needs to get married
A woman who fears Allah knows
Sinning is the greatest burden to
Carry

Don't tell her she is more beautiful
Without hijab because she already knows that
She is not oppressed or depressed.
Who sees her body? She controls that.

This piece is a very empowering piece for women who have decided to wear the hijab. In the threatening climate of Islamophobia, many women who wear the hijab are victims of hate crimes. Sometimes they are verbally, and even physically, assaulted. Nabila was physically assaulted and easily recognizable as a Muslim because she wore the hijab. Many women fear wearing the hijab because of the negative perception people in the West have about Muslims. Commonly, women who wear the hijab are challenged about their choice to wear the hijab, and many are told that they are oppressed. Many women who wear the hijab are stripped of their voice, not because they wear the hijab, but because they are told they are oppressed before they are given the chance to express their liberation.

VIII *Diamonds and Pearls*

You use to tell me I was beautiful
Until you saw other girls
Now I'm starting to feel as though
We are no longer diamonds and pearls

The more you tell I am beautiful
The more I feel insecure
Because a woman's beauty should be buried
Deeper than a diamond
But it is not anymore

We have become scattered rocks
Scattered all over the floor
So whoever wants us?
Simply picks us up
And when they see a shinier diamond
They throw us back on the ground

How can someone more precious than a diamond
Allow someone to toss them around?
The ideals of beauty are constantly changing
And so is the physical body
Thirty years from now
You might not recognize me
If you saw me

So why do I have to be physically
Beautiful in order for the world to
love me?
Is it because I am a woman?
And that is all the world can make of me?

You say your love is unconditional
Your love was never fictional
But if your love depends on the way I look

You would not love me if I was ugly

"Diamonds and Pearls" speaks to the mentality of a young Muslim girl, and how the society she lives in affects her perception of her body image. "Diamonds and pearls" is a metaphor for the beauty and charms of women. She shows her emotional pain at being appreciated for her beauty, until she grows old or a girl who is more beautiful than she is comes along. This is the concept that physical beauty is fleeting and internal beauty can last a lifetime. This poem also illustrates the importance of modesty in a world where the basis of female liberation is in exposing her diamonds and pearls. "Diamonds and Pearls" expresses frustration, pain, and love for women in humanity. It shows frustration because it depicts how worthy women are, but it highlights how unaware women are about their worth. It displays pain for basing a woman's worth solely on her physical attributes, and not also on her spirit, kindness, and personality.

VIII *Battling Insecurities*

Battling Insecurities
Feeling a sense of inferiority
Trying to clear the obscurity
Now that you have reached maturity

Maturity is reached the closer
We get to purity
Purity was reached when the Quran
Became the cure for me

The cure is free but we seek
Expensive ways to relieve the pain
Unaccepting of our image
Hoping we can see a change

Allah stated in the holy Quran
"We have certainly created man in the
best of stature." 95:4

Yet we are still ungrateful to our Lord?
We still ask for more?
We need to ask Allah to forgive us

We need to stop criticizing appearances
Battling our insecurities and scrutinizing
Our differences

So that there will come a time when
We understand what our mission is

95:4 Verse in the *Holy Quran*

"Battling Insecurities" is a war that most of us face throughout our lives. Almost every one of us has insecurities or an insecurity. Insecurity seems to be a war against our own selves, and our own negative perception of self. Sometimes insecurity can stem from the perception of others; however, insecurity grows because we nurture it daily. Many people can relate to Nabila feeling insecure, but many people do not fight against their insecurities. Many of us tell ourselves we are not beautiful, we are ugly, we are not good enough. Many of us wish we could be more attractive, more intelligent, more wealthy, or more successful in regards to worldly success, because we feel this will make us happier and loved or respected by others. However, the best form of happiness is derived from what is everlasting, not from a source which is fleeting. Allah is everlasting.

VIII *Less Than*

When you are feeling less than
You want to do anything to feel better
Sometimes you do not only want to
Get high through drugs

But you want to get high through people
Get high through compliments
High through acknowledgement

You want to get high through somebody
Who can help you boost your confidence
But then shortly after the buzz

You still feel less than and
Internally depressed because
Only Allah can truly relieve your stress

"Less Than" portrays how many of us react when we feel down or less than we really are. When we feel low, it is easy to attempt to make ourselves feel better by seeking an instant buzz through drugs, people, and a false sense of love. What is more challenging for us is to think about why we feel the way we feel, and how relying on Allah, by reading the verses in the Quran which pertain to our situations, can comfort us. Sometimes we try to rely on Allah; however, if what we desire is not granted right away, we tend to give up easily. Many of us find it difficult to understand that this may be Allah's way of calling us back to him.

VIII *Self-Worth*

I think we set ourselves up
To be treated like crap
and then we ask the world
Why am I being treated like that?

We are constantly accepting less
Than we know we deserve
Hoping that it will give us what
We think we should earn

How can we expect better from something
We know that is less?
That is like expecting happiness from something
That we know is depressed

That is like expecting the truth from something
We know is a lie
That is like expecting money to easily fall from
The sky

When we know things of value take time and
Work before they add up
We chase the voids in our heart and we seem
To never catch up

Some of us think that our lack of self-worth
is due to bad luck and a lack of accomplishments
But our lack of self-worth is more so
A sign of our impatience and
A lack of our self confidence

The poem entitled, "Self-Worth," connects with the reader by explaining how many of us behave when we lack self-worth and respect. Many of us lack self-worth when we do not strive to make ourselves reach our full potential. When we do this, we, in turn, allow people to treat us in ways that are less than we deserve, and we easily allow this because we do not even treat ourselves with the respect we deserve. When we are used to not loving ourselves, and not treating ourselves with love, we allow people who do not treat us with respect and love to linger in our lives. We become attracted to these people because we perceive this treatment as acceptable and normal. When we fight against our negative thoughts and strive to become our best ideal self, we only allow people in our intimate life who treat us similarly to the way we treat ourselves or better.

IX HALAL LOVE

Halal Love

I want that halal love
The love born through the words of Allah
The love that will never die because I'm meeting you
In Jannah

So we do not say until death do us part
We love each other for eternity
The love where you don't need to
Test the paternity

Because you're my first love
You know the rest if you've heard of me
The love where we do not say
We just need a little more time
Before we make it halal

Because there is always a fear
That we might collapse
If we do not keep each other near
The righteous path

We are always reminding each other
Of our deen and our purpose
In a world that glorifies evil
and scrutinizes good

We still know our struggle is worth it

I am not claiming that we have to be perfect
But if we are righteous Allah stated in his verse:
"Our Lord make them enter the gardens of Eden
Which thou hast promised them." 40:8

So this is our motivation.
How beautiful did Allah create our love?
Yet we allow it to be controlled by Satan

Our greatest struggle is
To fight temptations
But if we are patient and fall in love

With Allah's revelation
I believe there will come a time
That we truly love Allah and his
creation.

40:8 Verse in the *Holy Quran*

Halal Love can be achieved when a legitimate union

between a man and woman occurs through marriage

In the poem, "Halal Love," Nabila expresses her desire to be blessed with *halal* love from Allah. She realizes, after Ahmad breaks her heart, that *haram* (illicit) relationships consist of nothing but instant gratification and heartbreak. Haram relationships also consist of hurting our relationship with Allah SWT. Her experiences pain her and inspire her to want to be married to a good man because she is enlightened about real love through her past mistakes and guidance from Allah. The poem reads, "I want that halal love. The love born through the words of Allah." This means that there is a desire to have pure love. Love that is born through Allah's command and guidance. Nabila is aware that love without Allah is not the best love. Nabila desires the love that is best. The love that does not end with death, but the love that will last forever because your souls will reunite in *Jannah*. That is the best love. *Halal* love.

IX *Imaginary Guy*

It surpasses the measure of
Beauty to impress you
A cutie cannot suppress you
This is why I respect you

You are so coherent with desires
and temptations
You do not come near her without
Building a foundation

Following the Sunnah and Allah's revelation
Believes in the unseen is diligent
and seeks patience

His presence leaves a message
For everyone to reach greatness
His essence is expected honesty
Is his innate sense

His aura leaves a great scent
He does not have to make cents
For people to know that he makes sense

If love was a lake, he would transform
Into an ocean in great lengths
If beauty was a bird's song
His words would be every girls
Escape nest

"Imaginary Guy" may be the desire of many women around the world. The man described in this poem is called imaginary because Nabila seems to fantasize about marrying a man with these characteristics, but she does not currently have a husband. She desires *halal* love, and she desires a man with these characteristics to be her husband one day. She is currently unaware that she is in a coma, and that this is all one very long dream. Nabila's dreams and fantasies seem to be amplified when she is in a coma, and she thinks of her experiences in the past, which shape her current wishes, dreams, and desires. Nabila remains optimistic that she will be blessed with a husband who will truly love her and care for her.

IX *Scholar of Love*

You wrote her letters with love
And you lead her with love
She struggled to find Allah and
You let her with love

With love,
You studied her desires and emotions
So you knew how she felt
Before her words were even spoken

"Scholar of Love" depicts a man who is dedicated to truly loving his wife. Nabila dreams of a man who will treat her with care and compassion. She dreams of a man who will truly love her and bring her closer to Allah. He writes her letters, leads her with purpose and dignity, and he also allows her to find her way to Allah, without force and without preventing her from finding Allah. Nabila's past experiences have allowed her to understand more deeply what she truly wants in her future husband. Nabila desires marriage, but she is not married. Allah blesses people with spouses at their appointed time.

IX *Amarya*

She asked for care and he
Gave her love
She asked for something rare and he
Gave her a diamond in the rough

She asked for his protection and he said I
Gave her the honor of seeking her parents'
permission for us
She even asked for his password and he **gave her the**
Ultimate Trust

Then when she felt he **gave all of his love**
She asked him why **he gave so much** and he said
When a man **truly loves a woman**
He will always **give more than just enough**

Amarya Hausa word translated to English as Bride or
Fiancé

IX *Ango*

He asked for intimacy she
Gave him her heart

He asked for support and she
**Prayed to Allah to pull him out of
The dark**

He asked for respect and she
Gave him the best

She honors him in his absence and his
Deen she protects

Ango Hausa word translated to English as Groom or
Fiancé

While Nabila is in a coma, she has a dream that she is getting married to the man of her dreams and her prayers have been answered. She meets a man who is loving, caring, and fears Allah. They have a Hausa traditional theme wedding and this is why the word Amarya is used which is the word for bride or fiancé in the Hausa language. Her husband is very respectful and everything she prayed for. He is not only her dream husband but she is also his dream wife. We will have to see when Nabila wakes up if this dream will be her reality.

My Father once said:
"You should never give a man attention
unless he is willing to give you his eye."
At first I did not understand what this means
but now I understand that the only man who
deserves my love is the one who pulls his eyes
out of their sockets and sticks them to the
mirror of my reflection because he would
rather bleed to death than to look at any other
woman but me.

My mother once was advising my cousin
about men and she told her that when a man
calls you beautiful you should tell him:
"I know." When you say I know I'm beautiful
Now what? Most men usually do not know
where to go from there. They are so use to
women being insecure some feel all they have
to do is say you are beautiful to make you feel
good by using flattery. Some believe this will
make it easier for them to have their way with
you. I learned from the advice my mother
gave to my cousin that many men will use
flattery to get a woman but a man with good
intentions does not need to use compliments
to flatter you because he will compliment your
entire life.

I want to show love to the people who hold in
their tears all day until they are alone to cry
out their pain all night. I want to show love to
the people who are asked: "Are you okay?"
and they utter out of their quivering lips:
"I'm fine," because they feel no one will
understand them, no one will care, or
someone will be happy to see them in pain.
My words may not comfort your soul but they
may help you worship the one who created it
and that is my purpose.
My purpose is to worship Allah
while I strive to inspire you to worship him
right along with me.

Stop saying your Iman is low
or you have weak faith
Faith is something you have
to keep fighting for
If you were stuck in the ocean and
could not swim
Would you just allow yourself to sink until
your body hits the ocean floor?
Or will you use your flight or fight
response to fight while begging
Allah to save you?
Most of us are drowning in the
whispers of Shaytaan
Most of us are drowning in our desires
We drown in sin and expect our hearts
to land on strong faith.

Some of us paint pictures in our minds
Of how we will never be stained on
Someone's heart. We have brushed off the
most beautiful art and carved in sad memories
Through molding the least memorable parts.
We allow the past to craft our future and
We get too wrapped up in our present.
We feel our presence is not valuable and
It is difficult for us to grasp our spirit has an
eternal essence. We dream of
Nightmares instead of dreaming of dreams.
We focus on the sting instead of
How great we can be if we
Focused on the honeycomb tree?
What needs to happen for us to actually live
and not die before we are actually dead?

During the thunderstorm
You did not see the rain which makes
grass grow
Your eyes were fixed on
The thunder
But thunder brightens up the sky
And then leaves it in the dark
So when people promise to brighten up
Your life
You expect them to leave you
With a broken heart

NABILA'S QUOTES

The umbrella never changes
The condition of the weather
So covering up your faults
Won't change you whether or not
We stay together

I could write a thousand letters
And pray that we stay together
And you would still turn the next page
Looking for something better.

The only pain I know is in your absence
It lingers in my heart
With no intention to leave
Making me wait for your presence to get
Permission
To breathe.

Through every heart break
You realized it was haram
With every mistake you made
The solution is in Islam

If you disobey Allah when finding love
You will meet many people
In your life
Who will create love stories
which will end with question marks
Instead of periods and they
Will make your heart bleed

I prayed to Allah for a man who
Would never hurt me.
So I knew you weren't sent from the heavens
When you chose to desert me.

I loved you a little more than you loved me
And that's exactly what made you feel
You were above me.

If you admire her because she's a woman of
God
Do not come in her life
and make her a woman of the devil
Then leave her when she changes
and claim that you're on a different level

He said to his friend:

I'm a simple guy akhi
I just want a woman to love me for me
I just want her to be attractive to me
I just want a woman who will wake me up
for Fajr and help me better myself in deen.
I want a woman who has modesty is shy and a
virgin.
That's all I ask for but that's so hard to find
bro. He said after wiping the last bit of beer
from his lips with his sweater stained with red
lipstick after the party that night.

Akhi translated from Arabic to English as brother

I don't care how long your beard is
And I don't care about how many surah's
In Arabic you have memorized
Tell me if I had glaucoma would my eyes still
Leave you mesmerized?
Do you fear Allah enough to not desert me
Because I'm thirsty but I can't reach
A glass of water because I'm paralyzed?
Because if these questions give you paralyzed
Thoughts I'm going to need you to wipe the
drool from the corner of your lips because
infatuation is a drug that needs to be analyzed.

Let's not try to work it out and burn the fat
lies you created
Because ever since you thought I was
sweating you
I really did not wait ~~weight~~ long enough
So my heart did not skip a beat when you told
me I'm not strong enough
I'm not going to feed you with sugar coated
words to make things taste better
I have other people who want to eat from the
palm of my hands and their' personalities are
way better.

NABILA'S QUOTES

You had a watch
But you never used your watch
To watch over my heart
So how could I remember the good times?
When it was bad from the start?
You never saw my light when I was trapped in
the dark I knew you were blind
and I was too kind to blow your candle out
When it sparked.

NABILA'S QUOTES

All you do is play mind games
I'm not an Xbox 360
but I can make a 360 and X
you out of my mind
because I don't live in a box
that's why I'm one of a kind

They say forgive but never forget
but if I remember
Everything you did to me
My forgiveness will become a regret

At times people feel they are
not worthy of love
When in reality at times love is
not worthy of us
Because the people who claim to love us are
not worthy of trust

Love yourself more than anybody
This will allow you to build a fortress around
your heart
That can protect you from settling for just
anybody.

Self-love takes time.
You have to constantly tell yourself positive
thoughts
You have to tell yourself I am beautiful.
I am smart.
I am worthy of the best until you believe it.

NABILA'S QUOTES

How can you allow someone?
Who didn't make you
To break you?
The only one who deserves your love
Is the Lord who will take you.

NABILA'S QUOTES

Don't try to fix broken people.
When glass breaks and you try to piece it
back together you end up
bleeding.

You left me so broken
I thought giving away more of my pieces
Would give me peace.

Whenever you go back
It only seems to hurt more
So why do you search for a blessing
In something that's cursed for?

I was told once that you love my smile
So every time I see you I want to cry because
The last person that said he loved my smile
Made me cry more than he made me smile
and I want my emotions to move in the
opposite direction.

NABILA'S QUOTES

Your eyes spoke the truth
But your mouth spoke the lies
That's why I believe you when you cry
But I don't believe you when you smile

Our relationship with Allah
Is the only slave master relationship?
Where the master continues
To give to the slave
Even after the slave has
Turned away from him

NABILA'S QUOTES

Allah's door is always open
But we still knock
On the closed ones

Evil: I will only hate you one condition
Me: What is it?
Evil: As long as you're living
Me: Why is that?
Evil: Because as long as you're living your sins
Can still be forgiven.

Why do you cover your hair?
Do you feel oppressed?

Me:
No I feel I am in the matrix
Dodging bullets of gazes
That could be staring at my chest
I feel I have X-ray vision in a prison
Filled with women
Who believe fulfilling the desires of men?
Is the only purpose that God with give them.

"So why is there a hole in the ozone layer?"
The sun asked the earth.
Ozone layer:
"All I wanted was to be truly loved
And they took advantage of the parts of
Me which easily get hurt."

NABILA'S QUOTES

Poetry is deep
With this art
The pen is my sword
That I can use
To take your heart
Rip it apart
And use the blood
As my ink
…
Now Boko Haram do you have
Blood on your hands?

You abandoned
Lily in the dark
Because you thought
Her seeds would never grow
But today her son shines.

You perceive your life to
Be a nightmare when
You may be somebody's
dream.

I have been blown off
So many times
I can relate to Smoke

NABILA'S QUOTES

It's easy to go astray
It's easy to go wrong
But we will continue to pray
And we will remain strong

It feels good to fall for you
But it doesn't feel good to die for you
That's why when you ask me if I love you to
death
All I can really do is cry for you

To feel loved
You have to give real love
You gave birth to hate
But you managed to kill love
You managed to kill the heart
And you claimed it was still loved
But your heart was never moved
So I suppose that it was still love

NABILA'S QUOTES

She wanted to feel beautiful
She wanted to feel loved
She wanted you to accept her
For who she truly was

What if the weather was dependent upon
our emotions?
I would have left you rainbows
To fly across
and you would have left me
Puddles to soak in.

Why can't we walk on water?
but we can walk on land?
That's because we weren't created to sink
We were created to stand
and standing up for what we believe in
Was always a part of our plan!

If we never had a good foundation?
How could we ever makeup?

How could you find the perfect match
If you never lighten up?

No one ever wants to catch you
When you're chasing them
But they always want to attach to you
When you're replacing them

Someone is praying for you
So don't chase after the one
Who ran away from you.

If your heartaches
And you feel the tightness in your chest
It's not the lost love that should be making
you depressed
This is the best time for you and Allah to
connect
You should call on your creator
This is the best time to repent

May Allah protect us
From hard hearts that beat
And blind eyes
That see

I want there to come a time
When someone asks me:
"Why are you glowing? Is it because
Of him?" and then I look down
At my phone and say no
It is not because of him but before
The person shakes their head in disbelief
I point my index finger up to the sky
and say it is because of Him. Allah SWT.

ABOUT THE AUTHOR

Hawa Fuseini is a Nigerian and Ghanaian Muslim poet who began writing poetry at the age of nine years old. She was encouraged by her fourth grade English teacher who told her mother to not ignore her talent for writing. Hawa began to write at a young age but initially she did not share her writing with the world. However, in 2013 Hawa Fuseini was selected as the Editor in Chief for Pennsylvania State University's literary magazine. In 2012 she worked on the Global Awareness Dialogue project which focused on improving the pedagogy in classrooms for minority students.

Hawa Fuseini currently writes blogs for the Huffington Post on primarily race and religious topics. She has performed spoken word at a variety of Universities in the United States. Hawa Fuseini has been invited to different countries around the world to perform her poems and inspire the world around her.

You can contact Hawa Fuseini through her
Social Media: Instagram: @hawafuseinispoetry
Email: hfuseini@gmail.com

Made in the USA
Middletown, DE
06 March 2022